This Little Tiger book belongs to:

_____

_____

_____

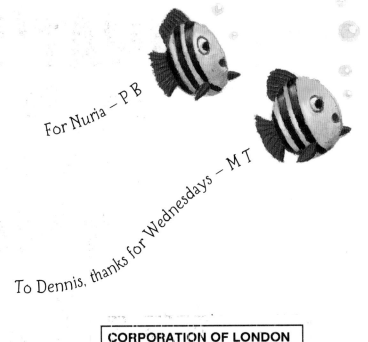

For Nuria – P B

To Dennis, thanks for Wednesdays – M T

LIT
TLE
TIGER
PRESS

An imprint of Magi
Publications · 1 The Coda
Centre, 189 Munster Road,
London SW6 6AW
www.littletigerpress.com
First published in Great Britain 2010
This edition published 2010
Text copyright © Paul Bright 2010
Illustrations copyright © Michael Terry 2010
Paul Bright and Michael Terry have asserted their rights
to be identified as the author and illustrator of this work
under the Copyright, Designs and Patents Act, 1988. All rights
reserved · ISBN 978-1-84895-031-3 · A CIP catalogue record for
this book is available from the British Library · Printed in China

2   4   6   8   10   9   7   5   3   1

WHAT'S MORE SCARY THAN A SHARK?

Paul Bright   Michael Terry

LITTLE TIGER PRESS
London

Shark was SERIOUSLY SCARY.
His eyes were dark and SCARY. His smile was
cold and SCARY, and his teeth were very, very
sharp . . . and SCARY.

If a young fish ever asked his mum, "What is
the SCARIEST thing in the sea?" the answer
was always the same: SCARY SHARK!

Only Lobster wasn't scared of Shark.
He was far too hard and tough to
be a tasty meal.

"YOU GREAT TOOTHY-GOB!"
said Lobster. "Leave us alone and pick
on someone your own size."

And someone Shark's own size was coming. As **BIG** as Shark, as **SCARY** as Shark. It was another shark, and her name was **Sadie**.

Shark stared at **Sadie**.

His scary eyes went *wibbly,*

his scary smile went *wobbly,*

and his sharp, scary teeth went

chitter-chitter-chatter.

"Lobster," said Shark. "Help me. I don't know what to do. I've gone all **floppity!** I'm in . . . LOVE!"

"Well, what a **SOPPY-SOCKS** you are," said Lobster. "Give her a present. Something girly, like . . . a bunch of seaweed."

"Just **ONE** bunch?" said Shark. "I'll give her **ALL** the seaweed in the sea. But if she doesn't like it, goggle-eyes, I'll scrunch your crunchy shell and use your claws for toothpicks!"

Shark raced here and there.
He found green seaweed,
red seaweed, thin and
stringy seaweed, flat and
flapping seaweed.

He arranged it all into a big, big
bunch, then swam nervously
towards **Sadie**.

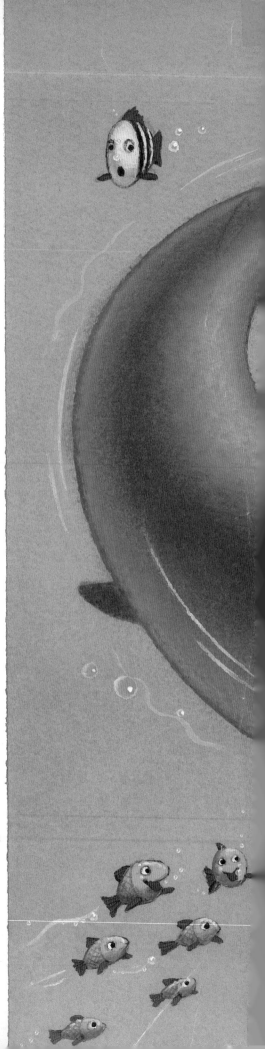

But the bunch of seaweed was SO BIG, he couldn't see anything. He bashed into a rock with a

CRASH!

and **Sadie** didn't notice him at all.

"The seaweed didn't work," said Shark, frantically. "What do I do NOW?"

Lobster thought hard. "What you need,
BARNACLE-BRAIN, is a pearl," he said.
"Find her a big, sparkly pearl!"

"Big? Sparkly?" said Shark. "I'll give her
the BIGGEST, SPARKLIEST
pearl in the whole ocean! But if she
doesn't like it, clunky-claws, it's
lobster and seaweed salad
for tea!"

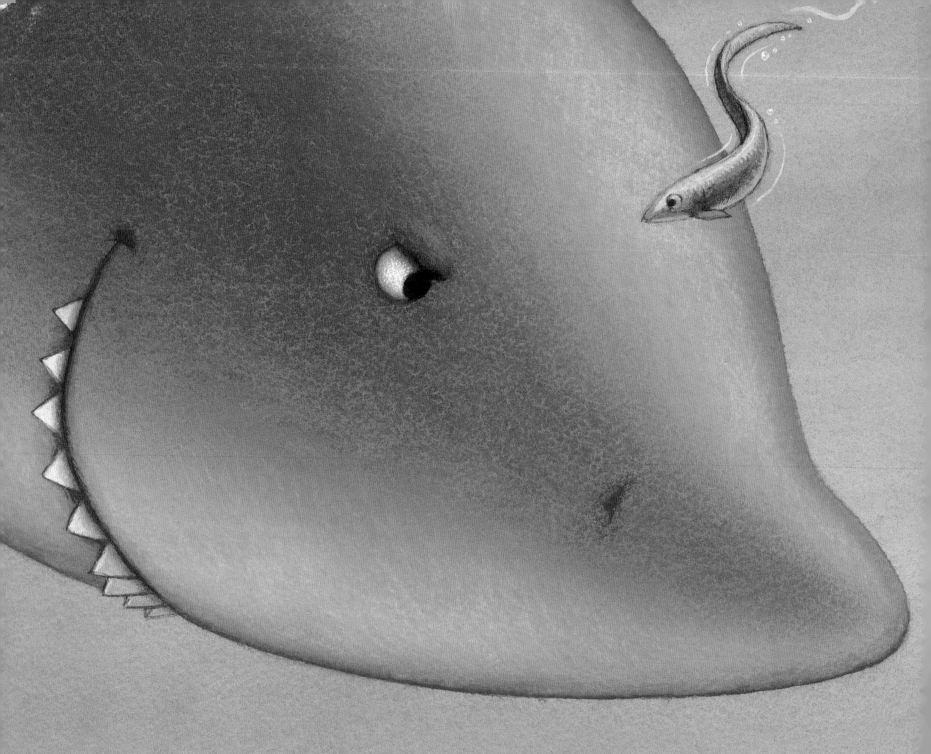

Shark searched until he found the BIGGEST
oyster, with the BIGGEST, SPARKLIEST
pearl in the whole ocean. Shark asked for the pearl
as politely as a shark can: "Give me your pearl or
I'll SPLAT you!"
"No!" said the oyster. "It's mine!"

So Shark reached in to grab the pearl with his teeth. But the oyster shut her shell with a

SNAP!

right on his nose.

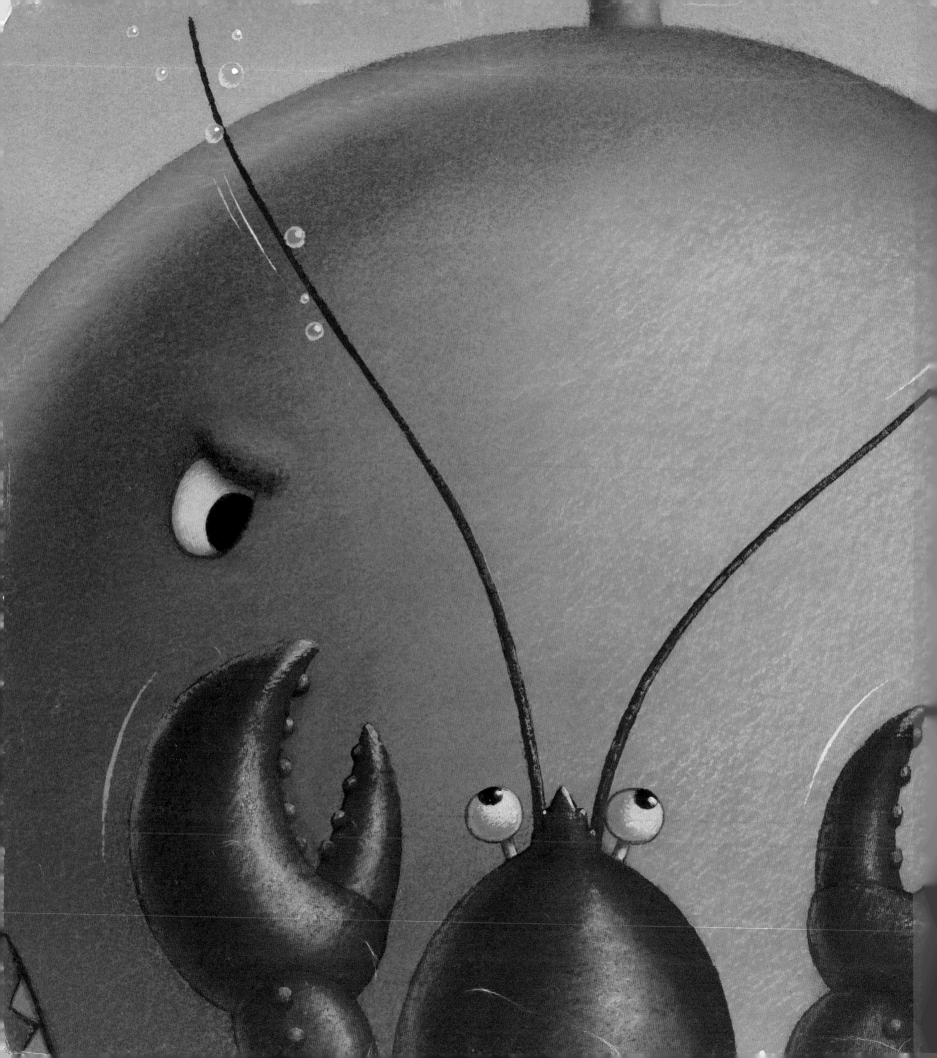

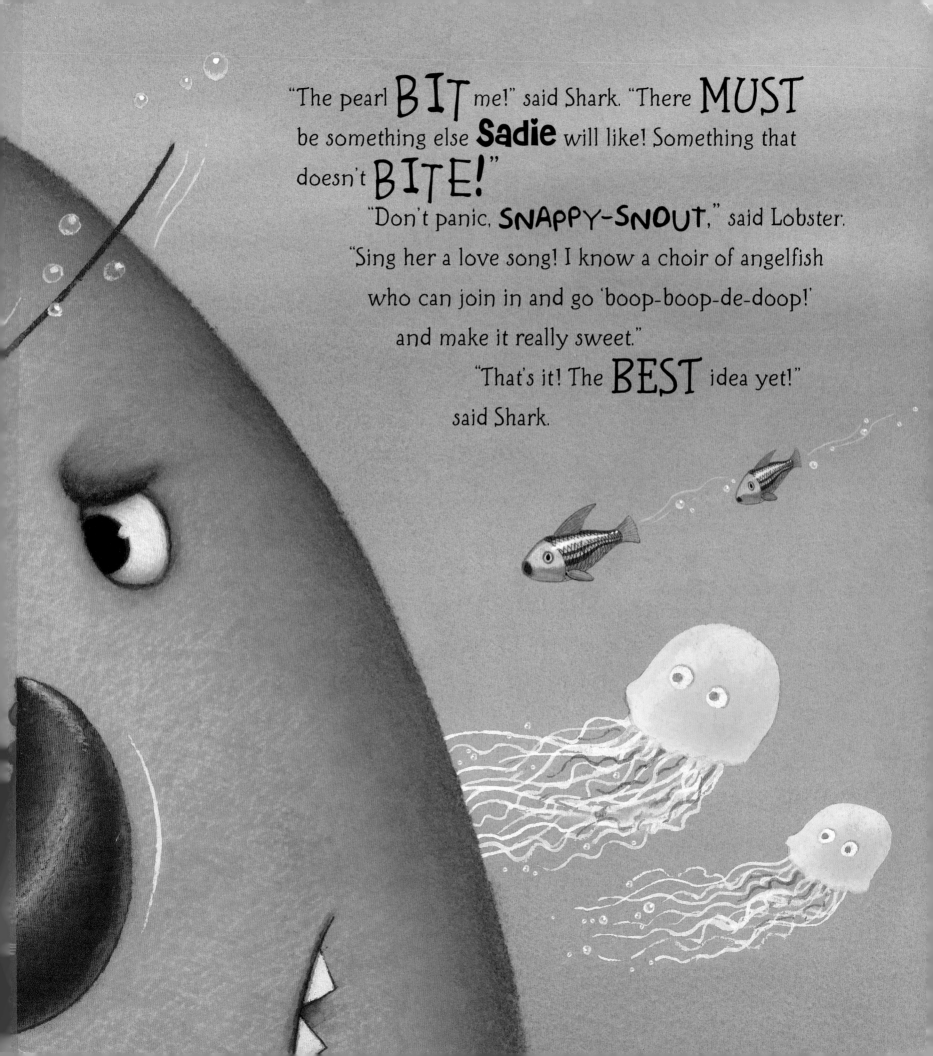

"The pearl **BIT** me!" said Shark. "There **MUST** be something else **Sadie** will like! Something that doesn't **BITE!**"

"Don't panic, **SNAPPY-SNOUT,**" said Lobster. "Sing her a love song! I know a choir of angelfish who can join in and go 'boop-boop-de-doop!' and make it really sweet."

"That's it! The **BEST** idea yet!" said Shark.

Shark started to do some singing exercises:

"LA LA LA LAAA!"

he sang, very loudly.

"LO LO LO LOOO!"

he sang, very softly.

Lobster hurried off, then came back with the angelfish. They were very scared of Shark, but did as they were told and swam into position near to **Sadie**.

Shark started to sing: "You make
my heart go *bibbly-bobbly!*"
And the angelfish joined
in, so, so sweetly:
"Boop-boop-de-doop!"

"You make my

heart go **bibbly-bobbly!**"

Boop-boop-de-doop!

Boop-boop-de-doop!

Boop-boop-de-doop!

Boop-boop-de-doop!

Boop-boop-de-doop!

Boop-boop-de-doop!

Then at last **Sadie** turned, and smiled.
Shark gasped with joy, and felt his heart
going more **bibbly-bobbly** than ever.
He sang again: "You make my fins go
wibbly-wobbly!" And to his delight,
Sadie swam closer and closer and . . .

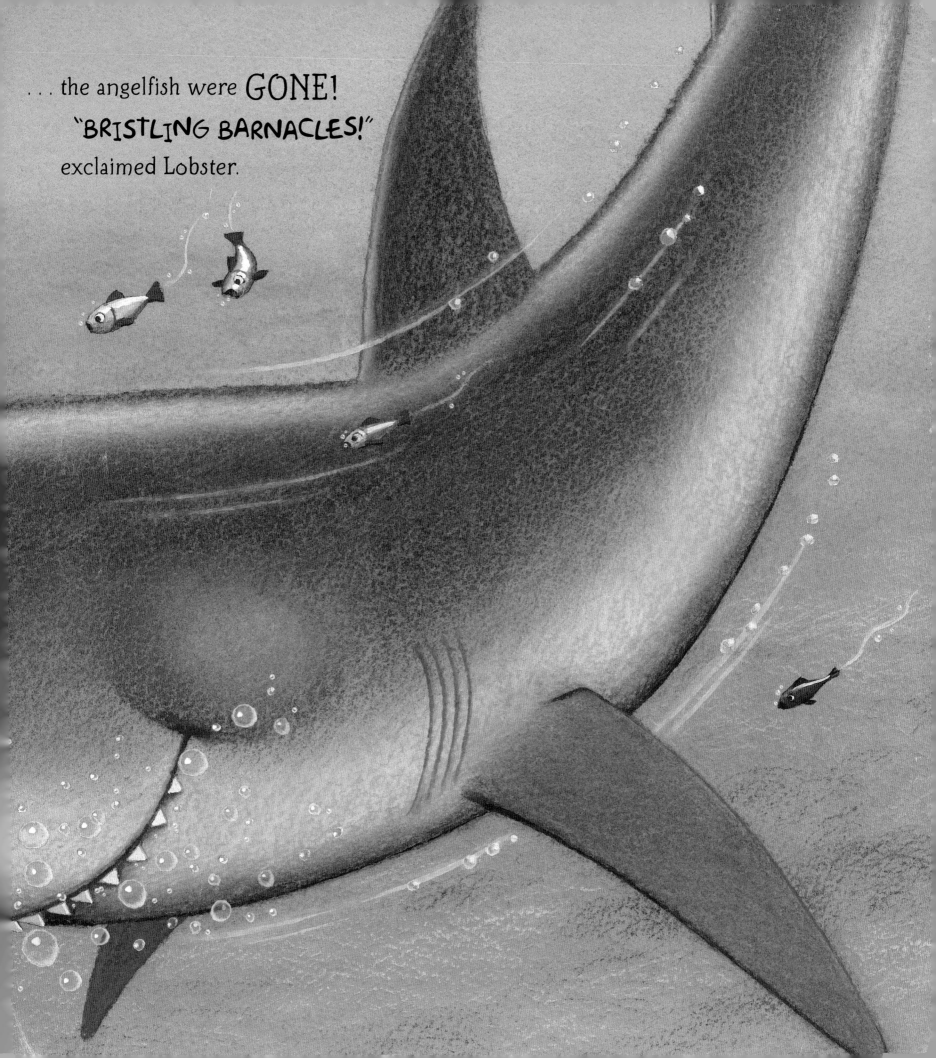

. . . the angelfish were GONE!
"BRISTLING BARNACLES!"
exclaimed Lobster.

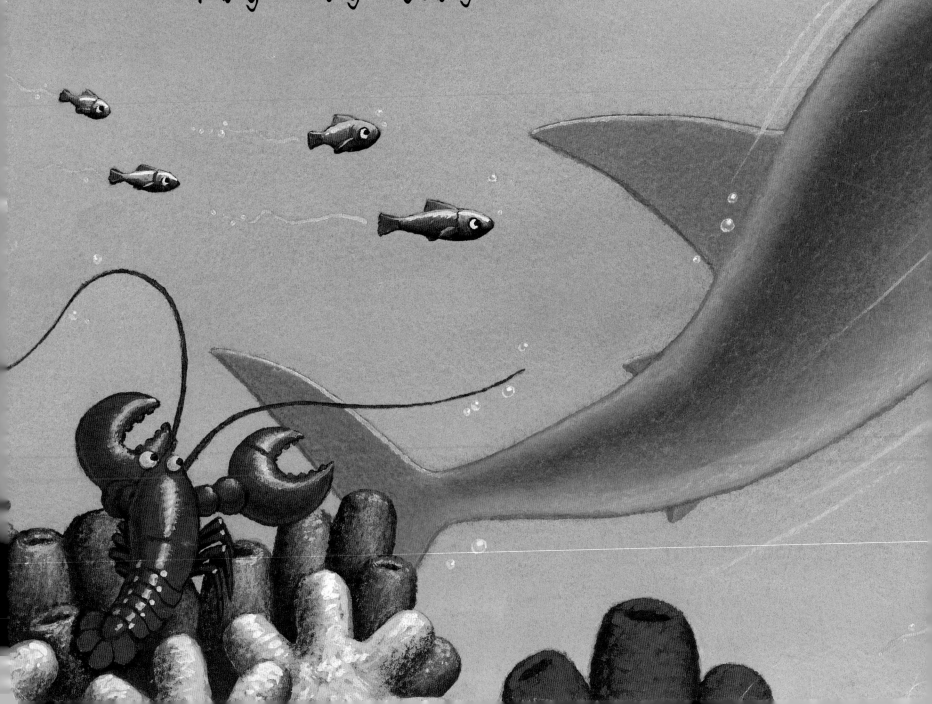

"What a lovely present," said **Sadie**. "They were delicious!"

"Wow!" said Shark. "You are the SCARIEST!

Will you be my own SCARY SWEETHEART?"

"I will," said **Sadie**.

They touched noses, and Shark's heart went all bibbly-bibbly-bobbly, and **Sadie's** fins went all wibbly-wibbly-wobbly.

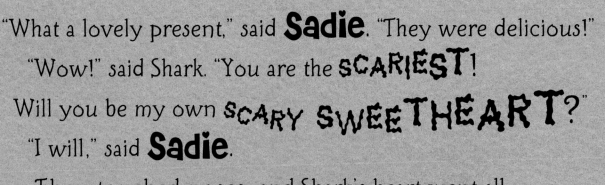

Then they swam off, **SERIOUSLY SCARY**, together.

Rhino's Great BIG Itch!

Natalie Chivers

The Great Monster Hunt

Norbert Landa
Tim Warnes

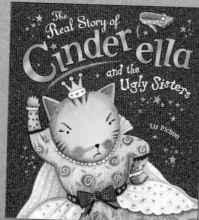

The Real Story of Cinderella and the Ugly Sisters

Liz Pichon

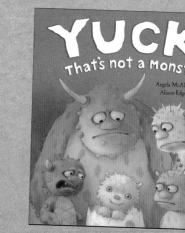

YUCK! That's not a monster!

Angela McAllister
Alison Edgson

You'll go bibbly-bobbly over these new reads from Little Tiger Press!

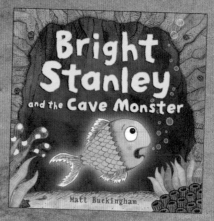

Bright Stanley and the Cave Monster

Matt Buckingham

THE GRUNT AND THE GROUCH

Tracey Corderoy · Lee Wildish

For information regarding any of the above titles
or for our catalogue, please contact us:
Little Tiger Press, I The Coda Centre, 189 Munster Road, London SW6 6AW
Tel: 020 7385 6333 • Fax: 020 7385 7333
E-mail: info@littletiger.co.uk • www.littletigerpress.com